For Rosie and Raffi – N.K.

EGMONT
We bring stories to life

First published in Great Britain 2011 by Egmont UK Limited
This edition published 2018 by Dean,
an imprint of Egmont UK Limited,
The Yellow Building, 1 Nicholas Road, London, W11 4AN
www.egmont.co.uk

Text and illustrations copyright © Nicola Killen 2011
Nicola Killen has asserted her moral rights.

ISBN 978 0 6035 7569 3
70169/001
Printed in Malaysia

A CIP catalogue record for this title is available from the British Library.

Egmont takes its responsibility to the planet and its inhabitants very seriously.
All the papers we use are from well-managed forests run by responsible suppliers.

Nicola Killen

Fluff and Billy

do everything together!

EGMONT

I'm climbing up! said Fluff.

I'm climbing up! said Billy.

I'm sliding down! said Fluff.

I'm sliding down! said Billy.

AAAAAAAAAAAAAA

screamed Billy.

AAAAAAAAAAA

AAAAAAAAAHH!

screamed Fluff.

AAAAAAAAAAAHH!

I'm swimming!

said Fluff.

I'm swimming!

said Billy.

I'm splashing!

said Fluff.

I'm splashing!

said Billy.

I'm running over here!

said Fluff.

I'm running over here!

said Billy.

I'm jumping up!

said Fluff.

I'm jumping up!

said Billy.

I'm rolling a snowball!

said Fluff.

I'm throwing a snowball!

said Billy.

OUCH!

cried Fluff.

I'm not talking to you!

said Fluff.

I'm not
talking
to you!

said Billy.

Fluff said
nothing.

Billy said

nothing.

I'm tickling your tummy!

said Fluff.

I'm... ...tickling

...your

...tuh

...huh

...meee!

laughed Billy.

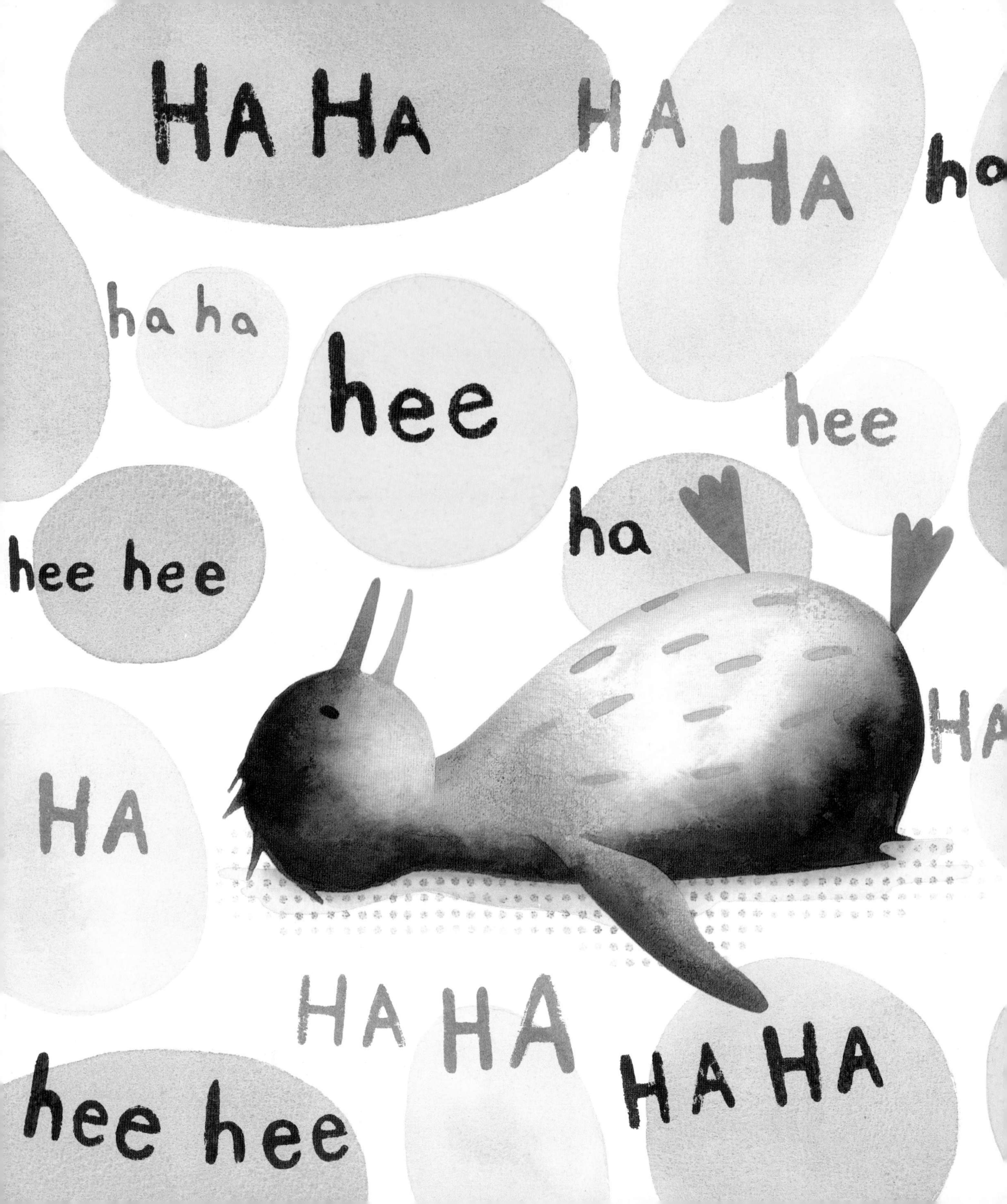
HA HA
HA
HA
ha ha
hee
hee
ha
hee hee
HA
HA HA
HA HA
hee hee

ha hee hee HA HA

HA HA ha ha HEE

hee

HA ha ha ha ha ha HA HA

HEE HEE HEE laughed Fluff and Billy...

...together!